I0763563

ZIGGY ZIG-ZAGS
THE LIGHT AND DARK FANTASTIC
BY RON BAXLEY JR.
Art by VINCENT MYRAND

Ziggy Zig-Zags the Light and Dark Fantastic, Volume 1

Written By

Ron Baxley, Jr.

Art By

Vincent Myrand

Layout and Lettering By

Ali Tavakoly

For Permission requests, write to:

YBR Publishing, LLC
PO Box 4904
Beaufort SC 29903-4904
contact@ybrpub.com
843-597-0912

ISBN: 0-9980582-9-7
ISBN-13: 978-0-9980582-9-0

Cover art by Vincent Myrand
Cover design and Interior formatting by Jack Gannon www.ybrpub.com

FOREWORD

BY

MARC BAUM

From Neverland to Wonderland to Oz, you're never really far away from man's best friend. Ziggy the Corgi takes us on an original adventure written by science-fiction and Oz author Ron Baxley, Jr., with illustrations by Vincent Myrand.

The delightful tale of a helpful hound will enchant you as the graphic novel pulls you in. Myrand's art is second to none, and the way that he makes the pictures feel like you can reach out and pet Ziggy yourself does not go unnoticed. Each illustration would be suitable for framing.

Baxley and Myrand have pulled together the magical lands we have all dreamt of, whether we started our fantasy adventure by going down a rabbit hole, with some Pixie Dust, or by traveling over a rainbow. In the spirit of fan rewrites of the classics, Ziggy takes us to places that are totally familiar, but gives us stories that are unique and fresh.

The magic of ZIGGY ZIG-ZAGS THE LIGHT AND DARK FANTASTIC is that we get to go along for the ride from the real world to the lands of our dreams and then back again. Ziggy and his friends have an adventure, and we have a front row seat. Hold on tight, pet the Corgi, and get your seatbelt on…the ride is about to begin.

Marc Baum is a founding member of the International L. Frank Baum & All Things Oz Historical Foundation as well as being a published author and host of an internationally syndicated radio station. http://www.allthingsoz.org/

Just like he and others once did for the Welsh elves, Ziggy, a Pembroke Welsh Corgi, was to serve as a steed for shrunken-down people and creatures from other fantastic lands in our world and even beyond our world, worlds light and worlds dark.

Once upon their backs, Corgis like Ziggy carried the elves into battle and through the woods for common domestic tasks, serving as their horses.

Hence, the Corgis to this day have bizarre white markings around their necks and faces. This is where the elven saddles and stirrups once sat and left their literal marks.

The Corgis wore their saddles and stirrups, by the way, during the Great Botanical Battle of the Welsh Woods when the Dark Elf usurped the throne of the Elf King, Appoli while he was away on a journey. The Dark Elf was defeated and literally and figuratively thrown out of the Welsh Woods, but that is a story for later.

Our story starts with Ziggy once upon a not too distant time and eventually in many once upon a times in many fantastic worlds...

Ziggy, through some pixie dust given to him by the elves and thinking happy thoughts,
flew to the second star to the right and straight on to morning to
Neverland. Ziggy soon found the huge treehouse of the Lost Boy, Tiddle, he was meant
to rescue.The Corgi wore a silver dog tag with elven runes for
valor and even the smaller elven runes for anxiety running perpendicularly beside valor.
This is a great honor.
Besides, just because I'm nervous
doesn't mean I'm not brave.
In this world, dogs could not speak in human language,
but Tiddle was expecting Ziggy from a message
from the elves sent
to Tinker Bell and the faeries.

I hope this works.

Elf-reka! It worked!.

Meanwhile, Ziggy had hidden his saddle beneath a nearby oak tree
to conceal his secret identity. He had buried it there.
Ziggy retrieved his saddle as a super hero sometimes does his costume.
Soon, I really will be
up, up, and away...

Around one paw, with a leather band, Ziggy had a separate container full of just pixie dust. He bit this container open and flung the pixie dust on his canine torso. He wagged his stubby tail and yipped.
I am so very nervous that this will all work out. We must press on, try, and fly!
This dog loves me... I remember a family loving me too... Besides... fun... adventures are ahead!
Soon, with happy thoughts, the Lost (Found) Boy was flying as was the Corgi. They flew together...

Unexplained floating daggers nearly hit them both. Not seeing anything, Ziggy, with Tiddles riding on his back, flew away from Neverland and on to a portal to London, England.
Zoooooooom!
Be brave. God-speed. No nervousness now... PANT... PANT...
O-ooooooooo.... Aaargh!... U-u-u-u-u-uh!
The pirates' telekinetic powers had not been enough. By the way, all boys in Neverland never grow up; however, all pirates and men who come there eventually die.

Here we goooooo!

The pirate spirits were not as amiss as when they were after the buffoonish Hook was finally defeated once and for all by a giant crocodile. The pirate spirits worshipped the crocodile god of death. This god was also the Never-god of time that ate Hook's hand
and ingested a ticking clock. The scaly monstrosity eventually ate Hook himself! Neverland's pirates no longer followed the false counsel of a bad man but that of a want-to-be evil god. They asked that he, Croc-Toc, adjust time to defeat Ziggy.
Fools! Idiots! I will deal with it! It is already planned in time. Warn the goblins down here, though,
and tell them to pass the word to other worlds! If Ziggy escapes, I will chew on your very spirits themselves as a hell worm does!

The darn runt
is zig-zagging between worlds!
The nefarious word of Ziggy's rescuing was
indeed passed on by the pirate spirits ...

Gossip of Ziggy also passed from demons
to some dwarves who chose to be evil
and to the Ice Queen herself.

"Mean-welsh" in London... .
Through the unseen evil powers of Croc-Toc, wicked god of time and death, the big hand of Big Ben plummeted suddenly, and Ziggy and Tiddle started falling...
Oh, no. He's panicked, scared, falling... Don't worry; no anxiety; deep breaths; think happy thoughts; think of a bone back home. Now to him...
Oh, no-o-o-o-o-o-o-o-o-o!
Tee-hee-hee!
Ziggy's ticklish licking did the trick to make Tiddle happy again and fly.

Ziggy caught the now flying Tiddle and zoomed him off to an orphanage in London, which was the destination the elves gave Ziggy all along.
Now that's what I call an adventure!
Such a good boy.
Ziggy deposited the Lost Boy safely in the main room of the orphanage. Tiddle changed his name from Tiddle to T.B. Pembrokenton, a pseudo-nym, an Oxford don specializing in children's literature and soon to be author of a series of fantasy novels in which good would always defeat evil. No wonder evil forces who could read the future wanted him dead.
As Tiddle had been away in Neverland for quite some time, where time passes very slowly for children, he began to age shortly after his return to London.
T.B., now a Found Man with ambitions to tell many fantastic stories of his experiences, hugged and petted Ziggy, wishing him a fond farewell.
Now these are the true rewards.

Ziggy next made use of the pixie dust to
travel over the Deadly Desert to Oz.
Ziggy was looking for the winged monkey,
Zephyr, who had a buzz cut,
among the other free winged monkeys.

The winged monkeys were no longer bound to the magic cap and its servitude. They no longer had to serve the Wicked Witch of the West. Ziggy discovered in Oz, unlike in the Out World and some other fantasy countries, that he could talk in speech humans and others understood.
We gotta go... go... go!
Ooo-ooo-eee-eee... Hold on. Hold on. Now we need to talk for a while. Ozma isn't going to move the barrier to the Out World until I call to her anyway.

Zephyr started his own tale of when
Ozma allowed the winged monkeys to leave Oz...
a tale told about a bigot...
full of zounds and fury... signifying much...
Dr. D.'s lab was located in a secluded area
near a lake in Kansas. No major highways were
near it which kept Dr. D.'s facility
from being easily located.
Once in the Out World, we winged monkeys discovered in America that a long-haired,
Arian blond neo-Nazi scientist, Dr. Disemblestein, had been experimenting on unwilling soldiers.
Disguised as a chicken processing plant
during a time when the doctor was experimenting
with poultry wings on people,
his facility kept its cover.

Dr. D., the crazed Neo-nazi, had been grafting flying squirrel membranes to blond soldiers to perfect an enslaved flying super-race!
(Zephyr strongly disagreed with humans becoming enslaved as winged soldiers, enslaved just as his comrades had been to the witch's golden cap. It stunk worse than flying monkey feces...and he ought to know.)

Those who often
go in the direction of the political are
often in the opposite direction of the
prosperous... at least they lead their
countries in less prosperous
directions at times.
Zephyr carried Ziggy and flew him out of Oz after
Princess Ozma opened the Great Barrier.
(Ziggy's pixie dust supply was depleted, and
the effect of the old one had worn off.)
They quickly flew across the world to some
small towns in Kansas to investigate
and to some direction signs there.
POLITICAL
PROSPEROUS

They stopped and looked at the simple, quaint shops of the village of Prosperous. They would have to think about what supplies they would need later and come back...
UMBRELLAS
It's certainly going to be.
Flowers
SALE
Ruff!
They decided they better quickly fly on to the secret facility not far from the outskirts of the village of Prosperous in a desolate, failed industrial park.
It is so good to have a friend, tried and true, by my side.
Be brave. It's okay to be nervous...

Just a... woo-woo... here... and a ... eee-eee... there... here a eee... there
Those traps were meant for me!
Deep panting now... calm... calm...
an eeee everywhere an eee-eee... Old Dr. Disemblestein had a plant... Ee-i-eee-i-o.
–Just about as bad as dodging old "Melty" 's broomstick all the time.
In the woods near the facility, there were booby traps low to the ground...

Ziggy picked a padlock on the gate on the fence surrounding the facility...
The elves never kept me locked up much. A villain did one time for what seemed like ages!
A laser system above the gate made it hard for Zephyr to fly over...
Once they were past the gate, Zephyr was able to fly Ziggy to each window of the big warehouse until they saw...
I quickly learned how to escape. Not many cages keep me!
I'll be a flying monkey's uncle if that sight still don't hit me.
A Corgi does not like to be tied down. I'm sure this fellow does not either.

Dr. D. was horribly nearsighted
and did not even see the two at the window.
Just a few more tests,
mein little soldier.
Moan!....
Groan!
Many blind people can be very kind.
He is blind in more ways than one, however.

The "fly-namic" duo quickly flew back to Prosperous to get their supplies. They snuck in after dark using Ziggy's padlock skills, took what they needed, and left money and a note in monkey scrawl. Chicken scratch seemed inappropriate.

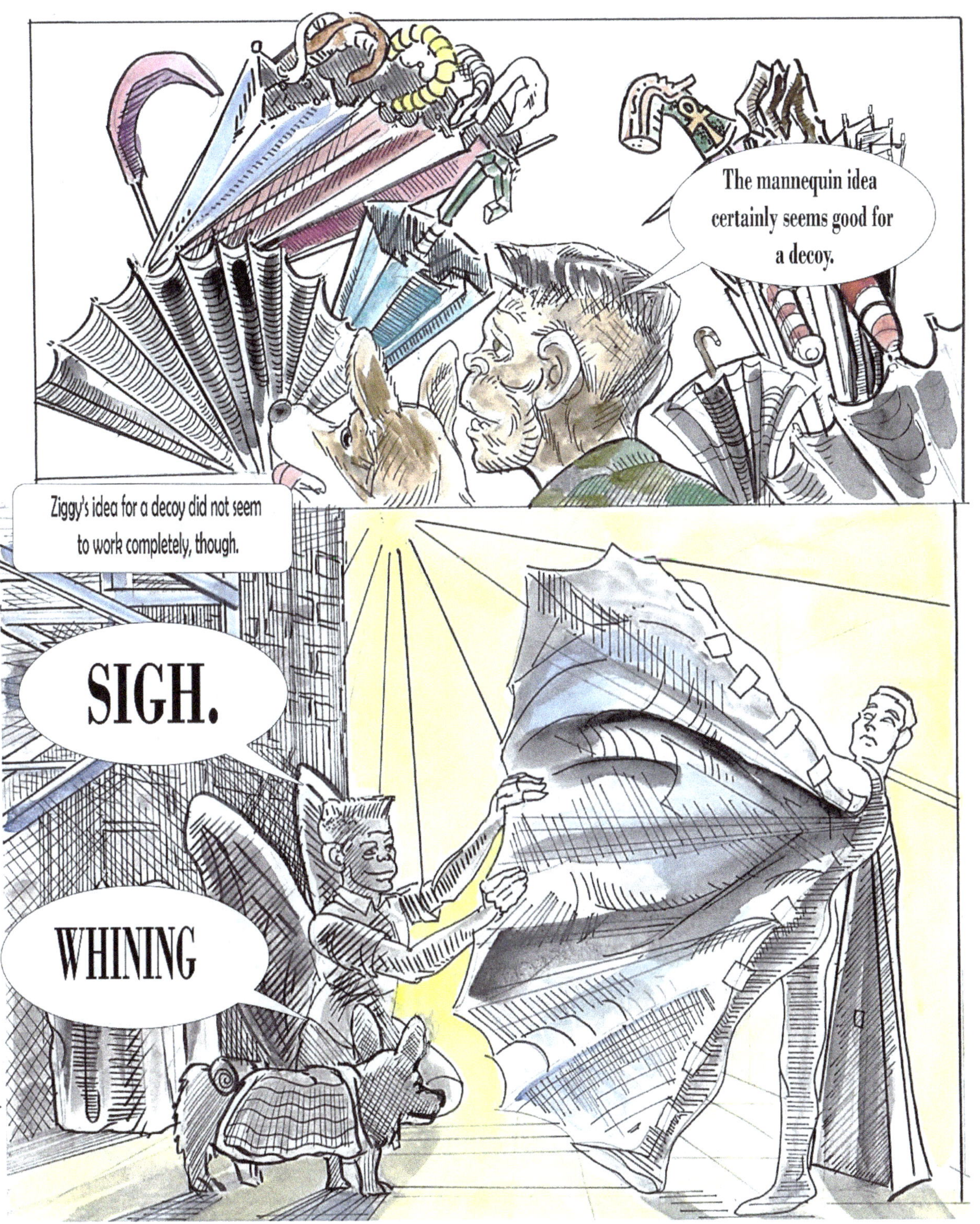
The mannequin idea certainly seems good for a decoy.
Ziggy's idea for a decoy did not seem to work completely, though.
SIGH.
WHINING

Ziggy and Zephyr had to wait another day, but unfortunately, the darker forces exerted their influence and came after them...
Run, Ziggy! Run!... That jerk is going way too fast!
Yikes! I... was... stumblin'.
Watch that oak branch!
YIP!

The Prince of Winds is after us.
Why didn't I think of this before?
They removed the wings from a dragon kite. They had left money for the dragon kite and a note again.

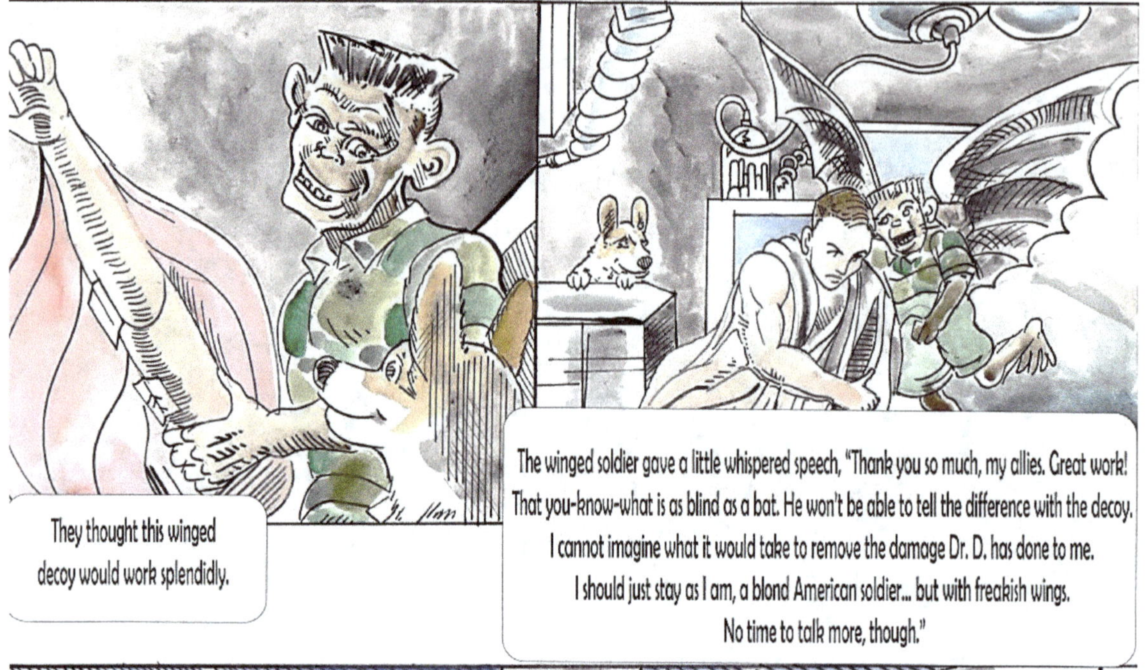
They thought this winged decoy would work splendidly.
The winged soldier gave a little whispered speech, "Thank you so much, my allies. Great work! That you-know-what is as blind as a bat. He won't be able to tell the difference with the decoy. I cannot imagine what it would take to remove the damage Dr. D. has done to me. I should just stay as I am, a blond American soldier... but with freakish wings. No time to talk more, though."

I rather like your wings, I understand, though,
and you're very welcome, soldier! I agree... We need to go-ooo-oooo!
Ra-rooooooo!

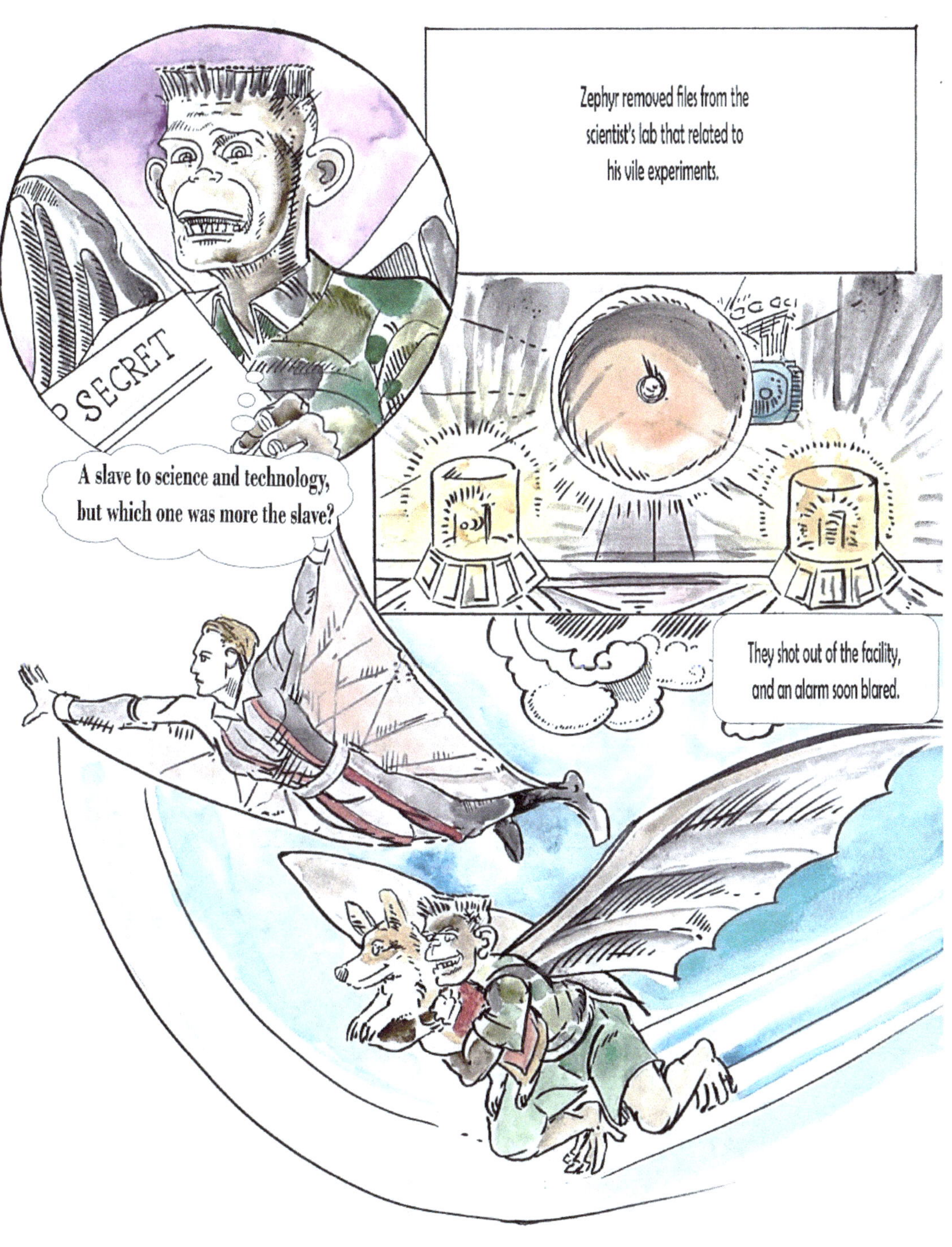
Zephyr removed files from the scientist's lab that related to his vile experiments.
SECRET
A slave to science and technology, but which one was more the slave?
They shot out of the facility, and an alarm soon blared.

ACHTUNG
Dr. D. thought the alarm was false,
turned it off, yawned, and went back to bed.
Their plan worked!

The blond, winged soldier would become a hero in Oz where he would fit in among the diverse, fantastic beings there. Ziggy had succeeded in his second mission.

Permanent marks, permanent purplish ebony bruises marked the face of the fallen elf, the Dark Elf, where he landed when he had been thrown out of the Great Woods years and years ago. He had his face lowered to the ground.

Before the fallen elf were statues of Croc-Toc, of the demonic prince of air, one of the dwarf who led the Evil dwarves in service to the Ice Queen, one of the Ice Queen herself, and the spirit of the Red Queen of Wonderland (even a great dragon was shown but in miniature). The statues were carved out of limbs of dark oak.

The Dark Elf spat, leering, "You who made all humans and lower creatures, I have put all gods before you. I have sent my power to them in order that they may work against your will. They nearly succeeded, the fools."

"When those thoughtless, brainless elves threw me out, they did not know what chaos I would wield. Then, they had to send their bravest steed, their most noble Corgi, Ziggy, to attempt to thwart my plans. The mulish mutt! He eludes even the dark gods as he ventures forth. Fear much, Creator, the dark gods will yet kill your champion and thwart your plans," the Dark Elf muttered.

"Not even Ziggy can thwart the plans I have cursed to the dark gods for him in the fantastic worlds. If he does by some odd chance in a trillion, I will kill him myself," the dark elf yelled and howled a dark prayer prostrate before his idols, idols he worshipped to defy the One Elf King Appoli worshipped. Yet the Dark Elf gave the idols his power yet also drew power from them.

Mean-welsh, Ziggy had to waddle his dumpy,
fluffy Corgi bottom in reverse through the Looking Glass to
to a secret location in Wonderland.

When Ziggy found the Mad Tea Party in Wonderland, he found a very pointy-eared, ivory-skinned elf in a blue and black tunic, an elf much shorter than the fallen one but similar in appearance arguing with the Mad Hatter and March Hare. He also discovered in the illogical country that all animals, including himself, could talk in human English.
Unbirthdays are not logical. To celebrate them is expensive. It makes a lot more sense to purchase presents on one calendar day if at all.
Unbirthdays are a tradition we are certain not to do without.
And certainly one we are certain to do within.
Mr., er, Elf, Sir, I can bring you away from this illogical country if you would like.
Discarded pieces of broken gold in bushes that had overgrown long ago, pieces of broken gold covered by some soil through time, began to emerge. These discarded pieces of broken gold were from White Rabbit's old pocket watch that the Mad Hatter had destroyed. These gold pieces started to transform...
What they transformed into will have to be read in Ziggy's next adventure. Also, find out if the logical elf can even go with Ziggy, discover what misadventures Ziggy will go through, and where the heroic Corgi may go to next as he attempts to evade the Dark Elf and his minions in Volume 2 of "Ziggy Zig-zags the Light and Dark Fantastic".

About the Author

Ron Baxley, Jr., and Ziggy, his Pembroke Welsh Corgi

Ron Baxley, Jr. submitted a skit to a glossy youth magazine when he was 16, it was accepted, and he has written for publication ever since. Having written stories with cartoons and poems for many years in his youth, Ron continued in adulthood to submit to magazines and journals with great success. Ron has worked as a newspaper reporter for six years in his life as well.

In later years, he added science fiction books and Oz books to his list of publications. He published the First Edition of The Talking City of Oz in 1999 (The Vanitas Press) which later appeared as a self-published Second Edition with illustrations by Gwen Tennille.

Ron was awarded a Lifetime Membership to the All Things Oz Museum by the International L. Frank Baum and All Things Oz Foundation in 2016. He has attended the Oz-Stravaganza festival that the Foundation runs in Chittenango. New York, birthplace of original Oz author L. Frank Baum, for most of a decade. He has also attended other Oz festivals and cons as an author. He attributes his success with books for children and youth to having been an educator for 15 years.

Ron also has a novel for young adults and adults which combines Southern literature with Oz fantasy, O.Z. Diggs Himself Out (YBR Publishing).

Ron earned in B.A. in English from the University of South Carolina in 1998. He took several creative writing and poetry classes in his major. He later returned to work on his alternative certification to teach English.

He has been a member of the International Wizard of Oz Club, is a member of the Oz writer and illustration group The Oz Inklings online, and was a member of the now defunct Not Yet Dead Poets' Society for many years.

For more information on Ron, please see his author page at: http://rbaxley37.wixsite.com/ronbaxleyjrofoz.

About the Artist
Vincent Myrand

Self-taught fine artist, illustrator, and art instructor Vincent Myrand has loved Oz for as long as he can remember.

Vincent's "The Wizard of Oz" and "Return to Oz" paintings have gathered worldwide recognition. He has devoted his life to the arts. Vincent was inspired by the movie "The Wizard of Oz" as a youngling, and shortly after discovered L. Frank Baum's "Oz" books. He fell in love with the characters and started drawing them.

He dreamt he would one day become an author or illustrator of Oz books. Membership in The International Wizard of Oz club helped fuel his passion for Oz (he joined when he was only 12!).

Vincent's passion for the Arts was recognized in high school when his teachers nominated him for The Haystack Art & Craft Institute in Deer Isle, ME, scholarship for that year. Also, Vincent was involved with the Bates College Gifted and Talented writing program. After Haystack, Vincent explored more art at Bates through part time art classes arranged by student outreach clubs.

In his early 20s, Vincent worked for Arts After School as an Art Instructor. Later on, he decided to open an art school of his own: the nonprofit Myrand Art Institution, which was opened in Maine in the 1990s.

In 1997, Vincent traveled to Italy on an artistic tour of Rome, Venice, and Pompeii, amongst other notable cities. Vincent already had a vast knowledge of Italian art and history. He has also been involved with the local music scene as a front man in bands. Finally, he has painted many album sleeves for countless bands.

About the Layout Artist & Letterer

Ali Tavakoly

Ali Tavakoly is a graphics designer with 16 years of experience, having worked for two of the largest comic book franchises, DC Comics, and Marvel, including the U.S. and U.K. versions of Masters of the Universe (2003-2004). He has been a regular exhibitor at Comic-Con International in San Diego and Anime Expo in Los Angeles. Tavakoly is a graduate of Irvine Valley College's paralegal program and has a Bachelor's Degree in Business Administration. He can demonstrate an interpretation knowledge of six languages, English, Farsi, French, Hindi, Japanese, and Urdu. He is a fluent speaker of two of them.

Please enjoy this sketch preview from

Ziggy Zig-Zags
the Light and Dark Fantastic, Volume 2

Author Ron Baxley, Jr. and the staff of YBR Publishing hope you enjoyed reading "Ziggy Zig-Zags the Light and Dark Fantastic, Volume 1"! We invite you to let us know how we did by looking up the book on Amazon.com and leave a rating and a review. Your feedback is always greatly appreciated!

www.ingramcontent.com/pod-product-compliance
Lightning Source LLC
Chambersburg PA
CBHW081137300726
48982CB00006B/988

* 9 7 8 0 9 9 8 0 5 8 2 9 0 *